# Goat Cheese

**Kelly Doudna**

Illustrated by Anne Haberstroh

Consulting Editor, Diane Craig, M.A./Reading Specialist

**ABDO**
**Publishing Company**

Published by ABDO Publishing Company, 4940 Viking Drive, Edina, Minnesota 55435.

Credits
Edited by: Pam Price
Curriculum Coordinator: Nancy Tuminelly
Cover and Interior Design and Production: Mighty Media
Photo Credits: Corel, Creatas, iStockphoto, ShutterStock

Library of Congress Cataloging-in-Publication Data

Doudna, Kelly, 1963-
    Goat cheese / Kelly Doudna ; illustrated by Anne Haberstroh.
        p. cm. -- (Fact & fiction. Animal tales)
    Summary: Nan Goat and her friends decide to express their own style in their school picture, but they have trouble settling down long enough to pose. Includes facts about goats.
    ISBN 1-59679-937-4 (hardcover)
    ISBN 1-59679-938-2 (paperback)
    [1. Photographs--Fiction. 2. Individuality--Fiction. 3. Schools--Fiction. 4. Goats--Fiction.]
I. Haberstroh, Anne, ill. II. Title. III. Series.

    PZ7.D74425Goa 2006
    [E]--dc22

                                                                                          2005027832

## SandCastle Level: Fluent

SandCastle™ books are created by a professional team of educators, reading specialists, and content developers around five essential components—phonemic awareness, phonics, vocabulary, text comprehension, and fluency—to assist young readers as they develop reading skills and strategies and increase their general knowledge. All books are written, reviewed, and leveled for guided reading, early reading intervention, and Accelerated Reader® programs for use in shared, guided, and independent reading and writing activities to support a balanced approach to literacy instruction. The SandCastle™ series has four levels that correspond to early literacy development. The levels help teachers and parents select appropriate books for young readers.

**Emerging Readers**
(no flags)

**Beginning Readers**
(1 flag)

**Transitional Readers**
(2 flags)

**Fluent Readers**
(3 flags)

These levels are meant only as a guide. All levels are subject to change.

# FACT & FICTION

This series provides early fluent readers the opportunity to develop reading comprehension strategies and increase fluency. These books are appropriate for guided, shared, and independent reading.

**FACT** The left-hand pages incorporate realistic photographs to enhance readers' understanding of informational text.

**FICTION** The right-hand pages engage readers with an entertaining, narrative story that is supported by whimsical illustrations.

The Fact and Fiction pages can be read separately to improve comprehension through questioning, predicting, making inferences, and summarizing. They can also be read side-by-side, in spreads, which encourages students to explore and examine different writing styles.

**FACT OR FICTION?** This fun quiz helps reinforce students' understanding of what is real and not real.

**SPEED READ** The text-only version of each section includes word-count rulers for fluency practice and assessment.

**GLOSSARY** Higher-level vocabulary and concepts are defined in the glossary.

### SandCastle™ would like to hear from you.

Tell us your stories about reading this book. What was your favorite page? Was there something hard that you needed help with? Share the ups and downs of learning to read. To get posted on the ABDO Publishing Company Web site, send us an e-mail at:

**sandcastle@abdopublishing.com**

Female goats are known as nannies or does. Male goats are called billies or bucks. Baby goats are kids.

School picture day is tomorrow. Nan Goat
is bored with always wearing a cashmere
sweater that her mother buys her. She wants
to look different this year.

Both male and female goats can have beards and horns.

"I'm ready for a new look," Nan says to her friend William.

William tells her, "Some of us are getting together to color and style our beards. We'll help you do yours too."

Sometimes owners who show female goats will trim their goats' beards to make them look more feminine.

Principal Capra spots Nan and William with their wacky beards the next day. "Kids! Is that really how you want to look for the picture?" he asks with a sigh.

9

Goats have a strong herd instinct. They are more relaxed when they are around other goats.

Nan, William, and the rest of their class gather in the school gym. They are very excited and won't sit still. Principal Capra hollers, "Kids! Please settle down so that we can set up the picture!"

11

Goats are very curious. They use their sensitive lips and tongues to investigate new items, which makes it look as if they're chewing on things.

Nan is curious about the photographer's gear. She chews on the camera case. "For heaven's sake, Nan! Leave the photographer's things alone," Principal Capra scolds.

Goats were originally domesticated in western Asia. They are very sure-footed and love to climb.

William joins a game of king of the
hill on the bleachers. "Kids! Come
down here before someone gets hurt!"
Principal Capra cries.

Contrary to popular belief, goats are actually very picky eaters and will only eat clean food. They do not eat tin cans.

Principal Capra finally has had enough. He yells in his loudest voice, "*Please* stand in your places so we can take this picture! Then you can stay outside for an extra half hour of rock climbing after recess."

Nan and the other kids are so quiet that they could hear a tin can drop in the cafeteria.

Worldwide, people drink goat milk more than any other milk, including cow milk. Goat milk is also made into many varieties of cheese.

The photographer says, "Say *cheese*!"

As the kids bleat, "Cheese!"
the photographer snaps
the picture.

Nan and William butt
heads. "This will be the
coolest class picture
yet!" they exclaim.

19

# FACT OR FICTION?

Read each statement below. Then decide whether it's from the FACT section or the FICTION section!

  1. Goats wear sweaters.

  2. Goats do not eat tin cans.

  3. Goats pose for class pictures.

  4. Goats are more relaxed when they are around other goats.

ANSWERS
1. fiction 2. fact 3. fiction 4. fact

20

Female goats are known as nannies or does. Male goats are called billies or bucks. Baby goats are kids. 9 19

Both male and female goats can have beards and horns. 28 29

Sometimes owners who show female goats will trim their goats' beards to make them look more feminine. 37 46

Goats have a strong herd instinct. They are more relaxed when they are around other goats. 55 62

Goats are very curious. They use their sensitive lips and tongues to investigate new items, which makes it look as if they're chewing on things. 71 80 87

Goats were originally domesticated in western Asia. They are very sure-footed and love to climb. 94 103

Contrary to popular belief, goats are actually very picky eaters and will only eat clean food. They do not eat tin cans. 111 122 125

Worldwide, people drink goat milk more than any other milk, including cow milk. Goat milk is also made into many varieties of cheese. 133 143 148

School picture day is tomorrow. Nan Goat is    8
bored with always wearing a cashmere sweater   15
that her mother buys her. She wants to look    24
different this year.    27

"I'm ready for a new look," Nan says to her    37
friend William.    39

William tells her, "Some of us are getting    47
together to color and style our beards. We'll help    56
you do yours too."    60

Principal Capra spots Nan and William with    67
their wacky beards the next day. "Kids! Is that    76
really how you want to look for the picture?" he    86
asks with a sigh.    90

Nan, William, and the rest of their class    98
gather in the school gym. They are very excited    107
and won't sit still. Principal Capra hollers, "Kids!    115
Please settle down so that we can set up the    125
picture!"    126

Nan is curious about the photographer's gear. 133
She chews on the camera case. "For heaven's sake, 142
Nan! Leave the photographer's things alone," 148
Principal Capra scolds. 151

William joins a game of king of the hill on the 162
bleachers. "Kids! Come down here before someone 169
gets hurt!" Principal Capra cries. 174

Principal Capra finally has had enough. He yells 182
in his loudest voice, *"Please* stand in your places so 192
we can take this picture! Then you can stay outside 202
for an extra half hour of rock climbing after recess." 212

Nan and the other kids are so quiet that they 222
could hear a tin can drop in the cafeteria. 231

The photographer says, "Say *cheese*!" 236

As the kids bleat, "Cheese!" the photographer 243
snaps the picture. Nan and William butt heads. 251
"This will be the coolest class picture yet!" they 260
exclaim. 261

# GLOSSARY

**bleachers.** rows of raised benches for sitting on at sports events and the like

**cashmere.** the fine, soft wool from a cashmere goat

**contrary.** opposite

**gear.** equipment

**instinct.** a natural pattern of behavior that a species is born with

**king of the hill.** a children's game in which players attempt to get to the top of a hill or other high spot and stay there

To see a complete list of SandCastle™ books and other nonfiction titles from ABDO Publishing Company, visit www.abdopublishing.com or contact us at: 4940 Viking Drive, Edina, Minnesota 55435 • 1-800-800-1312 • fax: 1-952-831-1632